Rockets

SPACE TWINS

Sun, Sand and Space

Wendy Smith

A & C Black • London

Rockets series:

CROOK CATCHERS - Karen Wallace & Judy Brown

HAUNTED MOUSE - Dee Shulman

LITTLE T - Frank Rodgers

MOTLEY'S CREW - Margaret Ryan &
Margaret Chamberlain

MR CROC - Frank Rodgers

MRS MAGIC - Wendy Smith

MY FUNNY FAMILY - Colin West

ROVER - Chris Powling & Scoular Anderson

SILLY SAUSAGE - Michaela Morgan & Dee Shulman

SPACE TWINS - Wendy Smith

WIZARD'S BOY - Scoular Anderson

First paperback edition 2003
First published 2002 by A & C Black Publishers Ltd
37 Soho Square, London W1D 3QZ
www.acblack.com

Text and illustrations copyright © 2002 Wendy Smith

ISBN 0-7136-6114-3

A CIP catalogue record for this book is available
from the British Library.

A & C Black uses paper produced with elemental
chlorine-free pulp, harvested from managed sustainable forests.

Printed and bound by G. Z. Printek, Bilbao, Spain.

Chapter One

Deep in space, far, far away, flies the good ship Zazaza.

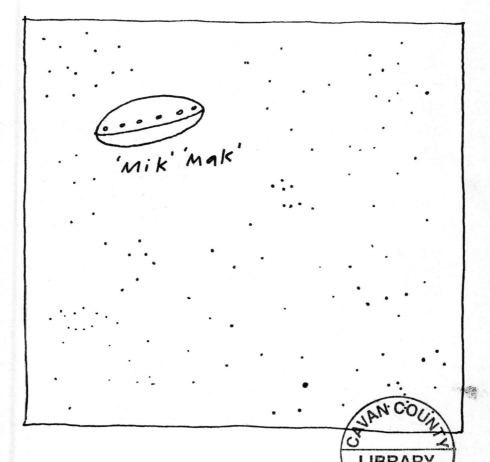

Each night it sends a signal.

Before they go to bed, Wilbur Day
and his Space Spotter Squad listen out
for the sound.
They are on the roof of Golden Towers,
the flats where they live in East Volesey*.

*a suburb on the fringe of nowhere.

Wilbur and his neighbours are
waiting to speak to their space friends,
the twins, Mik and Mak.

I've nothing much to say tonight, Mik.

Nor have I Mak. Let's not bother. Let's go to sleep.

Mik and Mak were feeling a bit bored and a bit lonely.

In the middle of the night, Mik and Mak woke up suddenly.

They crept out of their sleeping pods and made their way to the Clone Zone entrance.

Chapter Two

As soon as they entered the Clone Zone there was a great deal of clonking and buzzing.

A smell of smoke wafted in the air.

Little stars spun round Mik and Mak's heads.

Mik and Mak went back to their pods to sleep. When they woke up the next day they were not alone.

There were a lot of new faces in the
Gym Zone that day.

clones learning
how to move

But as there were no girl clones
Mik and Mak were soon bored...

...especially since the clones had
nothing to say.

It was funny seeing the Captain's cabin full of clones, though.

That night the twins went to speak
to Wilbur. The clones came along too,
and signals beeped out all over the sky.

Wilbur could not work out what was
going on.

But after a while the real Mik and Mak got through.

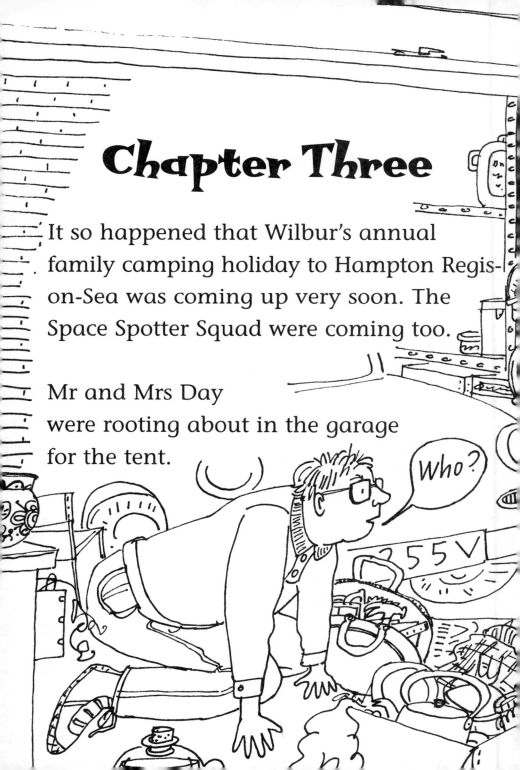

Chapter Three

It so happened that Wilbur's annual family camping holiday to Hampton Regis-on-Sea was coming up very soon. The Space Spotter Squad were coming too.

Mr and Mrs Day were rooting about in the garage for the tent.

Who?

I've been looking for this.
Would you mind if I brought some new friends camping? As well as Ted and Zigs.
Some nice boy twins.

Wilbur's mum and dad were more than happy for the twins to join them.

Wilbur thought they would all have a
great time.

Wilbur called the squad together.

They put the idea to Mik and Mak.

At last it was time to go on holiday.
Mr and Mrs Day set off for
Hampton Regis-on-Sea.

Chapter Four

Mik and Mak found it easier to get away than they expected.

There were so many clones that nobody knew who was who.

Cheekily, they stole away in
Captain Lupo's commutocraft.

They parked secretly in a clump of trees beyond Wilbur's tent.

Mr and Mrs Day made them very welcome.

Mik and Mak had never been
camping before.

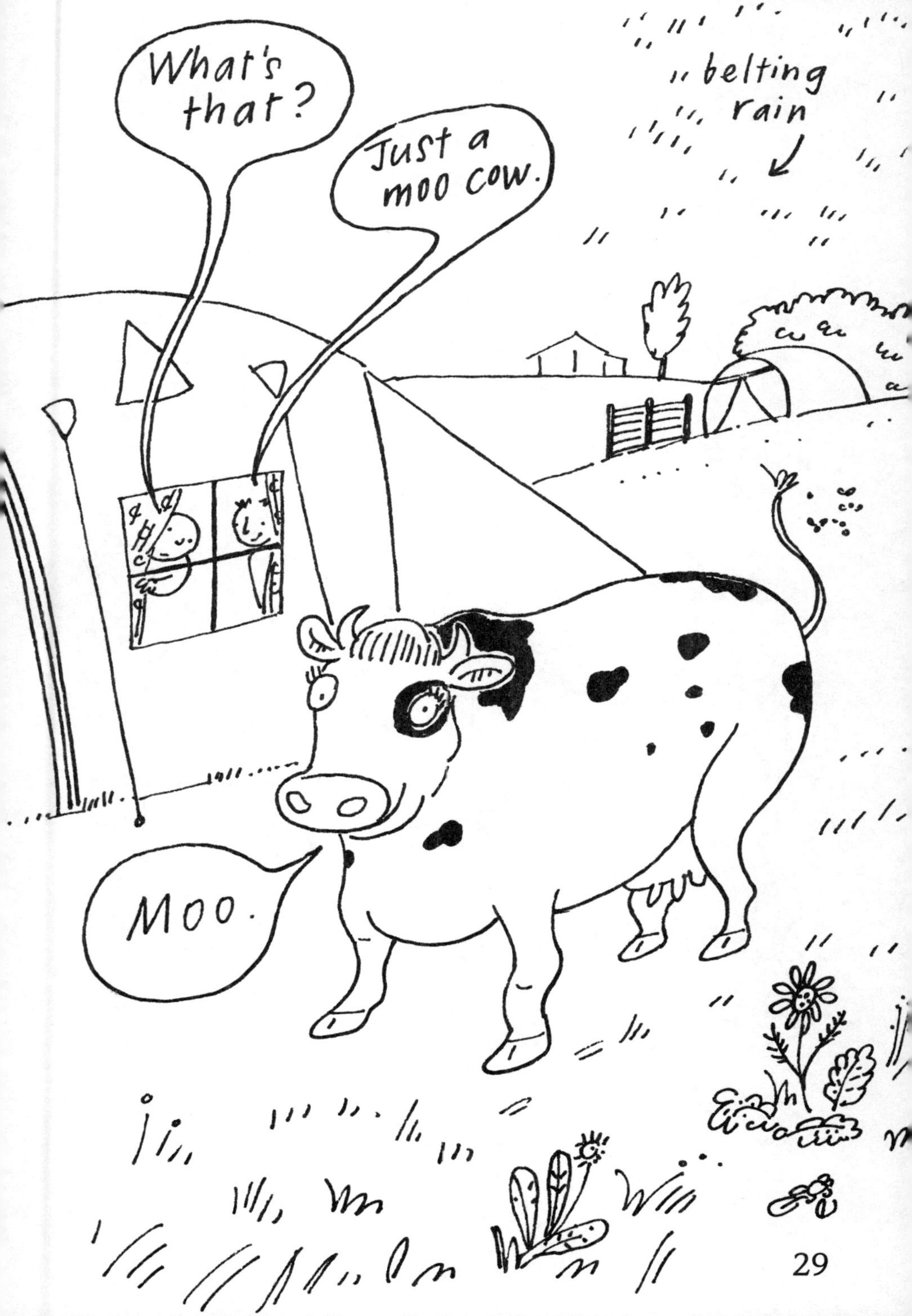
What's that?
Just a moo cow.
belting rain
Moo.

They hadn't been to the seaside either.

The twins found they didn't always agree.
Mik loved the food but Mak hated it.

Mik loved the crazy golf and
amusement arcades.

Whereas Mak loved the roller coaster.

But back in the tent they found
something to agree on.
The sound
of pouring rain,
cows mooing
and birds
singing
scared them.
Worst of all
was the sound
of people snoring.

And, between you and me,
they both felt space-sick.

Chapter Five

Back on the good ship Zazaza...

At first nobody noticed the twins were missing. But, one by one, the clones were coming to the end of their shelf life.

You can imagine Zuna's dismay when
she could not find the real Mik and Mak.

What should she do?

She scoured the ship in search of them,
but her search was in vain.

She located Golden Towers and
activated the voicer.

But try as she might, she could not make contact. As you know, Wilbur and the East Volesey Space Spotter Squad were away on holiday.

Luckily for her, Stan the Pie Man was making a late-night delivery in East Volesey when he picked up a strange signal on his mobile phone.

Oo's that? 'Ullo, outer space? You some kind of nut? You say two little boys called Mik and Mak have disappeared. I'll ring my mates.

Stan had a ring round.

As chance would have it, that night Stan's friend Big Bazza was going to the Hampton campsite shop.

It wasn't hard to spot the twins.

Wilbur, Ted and Ziggy said goodbye.

In the dead of night, Mik and Mak
leaped into the commutocraft
and jetted into space.

Chapter Six

Meanwhile, Captain Lupo had begun to suspect that something was wrong.

The clones were dropping like flies.

Captain Lupo went to see Zuna.

As they entered the Captain's cabin, an awful noise set their ears ringing. Mik and Mak were making a mess of parking the commutocraft.

boing!

Captain Lupo read Mik and Mak
the riot act.

All week Mik and Mak were made
to grade stardust – a fiddly job
where the dust gets everywhere.

But they missed their Earth friends, so each night they send a signal.